Zebra Stripes
Go Head to Toe

Sheryl and Simon Shapiro

annick press
toronto + new york + vancouver

Annick Press Ltd.

We acknowledge the support of the Canada Council for the Arts, the Ontario Arts Council, and the Government of Canada through the Canada Book Fund (CBF) for our publishing activities.

ONTARIO ARTS COUNCIL
CONSEIL DES ARTS DE L'ONTARIO
50 YEARS OF ONTARIO GOVERNMENT SUPPORT OF THE ARTS
50 ANS DE SOUTIEN DU GOUVERNEMENT DE L'ONTARIO AUX ARTS

Cataloging in Publication

Shapiro, Sheryl
    Zebra stripes go head to toe / Sheryl and Simon Shapiro.

(Shapes & spaces)
Also issued in electronic format.
ISBN 978-1-55451-581-3 (bound).—ISBN 978-1-55451-580-6 (pbk.)

    1. Stripes—Juvenile literature. 2. Square—Juvenile literature.
I. Shapiro, Simon II. Title III. Series: Shapes & spaces.

BF293.S53 2013   j152.14'23   C2013-900595-1

Distributed in Canada by:
Firefly Books Ltd.
50 Staples Avenue, Unit 1
Richmond Hill, ON L4B 0A7

Published in the U.S.A. by Annick Press (U.S.) Ltd.
Distributed in the U.S.A. by:
Firefly Books (U.S.) Inc.
P.O. Box 1338
Ellicott Station
Buffalo, NY 14205

Printed in China

Visit us at: www.annickpress.com

For our great-nieces
and great-nephews:
Dan, Ari, Jordan, Gavriella,
Ayala, Eli, Daniel, Netani,
Jessica, Rafi, Eitan,
and Dina—
great kids all!

A square has every
side the same,

and lots of them
can make a game.

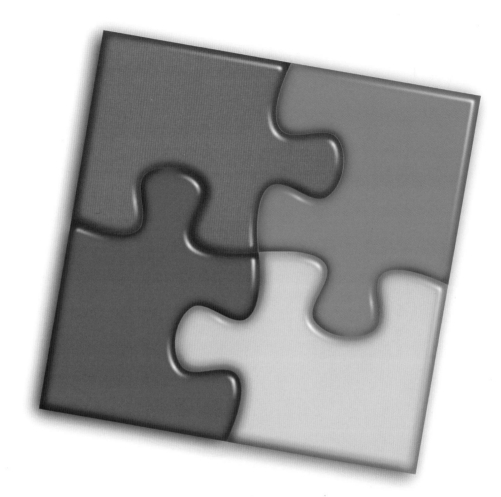

There are four corners
on a square ...

Oops—one's gone!
Do you know where?

1 2
3 4

This cube is stuffed,
jam-packed inside ...

This box has space—
a place to hide?

6

Which side up?
The blocks don't care.

On all six sides
you'll find a square.

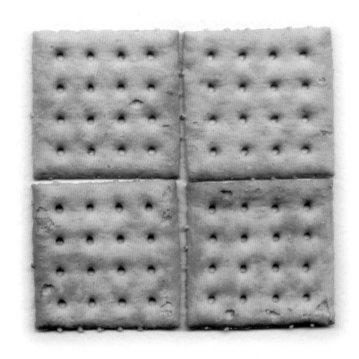

Crispy crackers
thin and flat,

cubes of cheese go
great with that.

Soccer nets are
squares in air;
so are windows—
don't kick there!

Some stripes run
from head to feet,

others go
across the
street.

14

Lines are thin,
stripes are thicker.

Forget the fork—
slurping's quicker.

16

Slats have gaps
for a nose—
pigaboo!

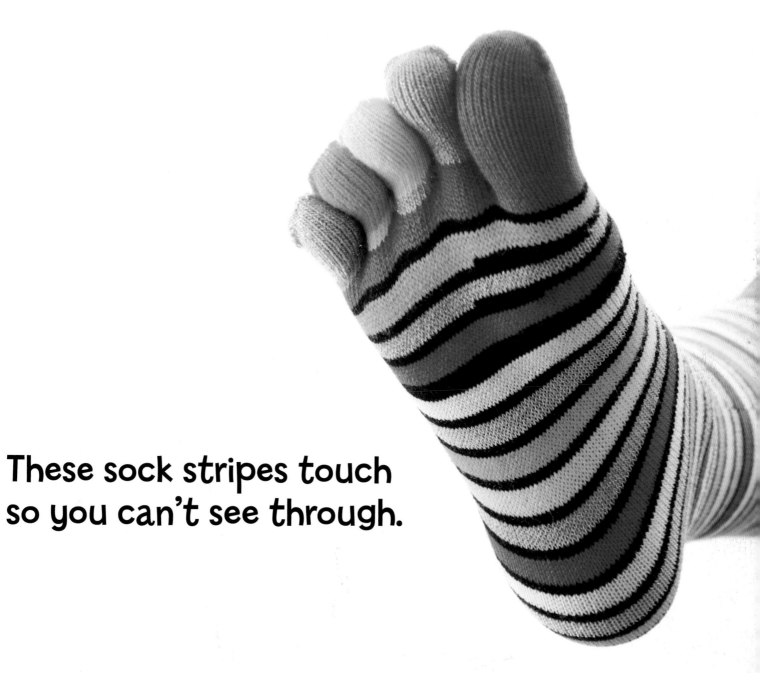

These sock stripes touch
so you can't see through.

18

The bands go whooshing
round the bend—

no start, no stop,
they never end.